This igloo book belongs to:

....

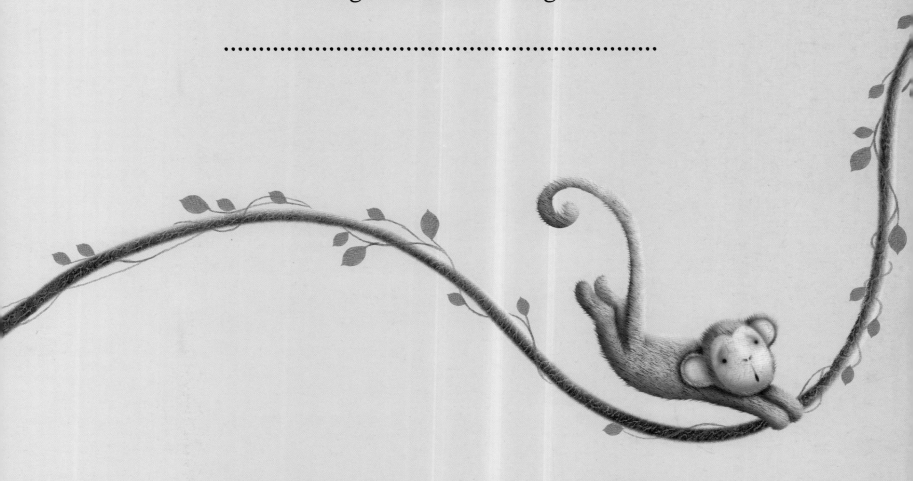

Published in 2019
by Igloo Books Ltd
Cottage Farm
Sywell
NN6 0BJ
www.igloobooks.com

GOL002 0319
2 4 6 8 10 9 7 5 3 1
ISBN: 978-1-78905-667-9

Written by Melanie Joyce
Illustrated by James Newman Gray
Additional illustrations by Nigel Chilvers

Printed and manufactured in China

Trumpety Trump

igloobooks

On a hot, lazy day in the deep, deep jungle, the animals were snoozing in the afternoon sun.

All except Little Elephant,
who swished his trunk and
went trumpety-trump,
trumpety-trump!

Trumpety-trump

Out of the grass, a snake came slithering.
She went **hiss, hiss** as she wiggled and squiggled,
following Little Elephant
through the jungle grass.

"What's that hissing and swishing?"
asked the parrots in the treetops.
They fluffed up their feathers
and they all went **squawk!**

In the branches of the trees,
the monkeys stopped snoozing.
They listened to the
trumpeting and the
hissing and Parrot
going **squawk!**

Squawk, squawk!

Hiss, hiss!

Trumpety-trump!

Oo-oo!

Oo-oo! they cried,
swinging their long, curly tails.

In the cool waterhole, the big hippos went **glug**, blowing bubbles as they bathed.

Glug, glug went Hippo and he joined the jungle parade.

Along the riverbank, the animals came
with a **trumpet** and a **hiss**
and a very loud **squawk**,
an **oo-oo** and a **glug, glug**.
"What fun!" thought Crocodile
and gave a very loud **SNAP!**

Oo-oo!

Glug, glug!

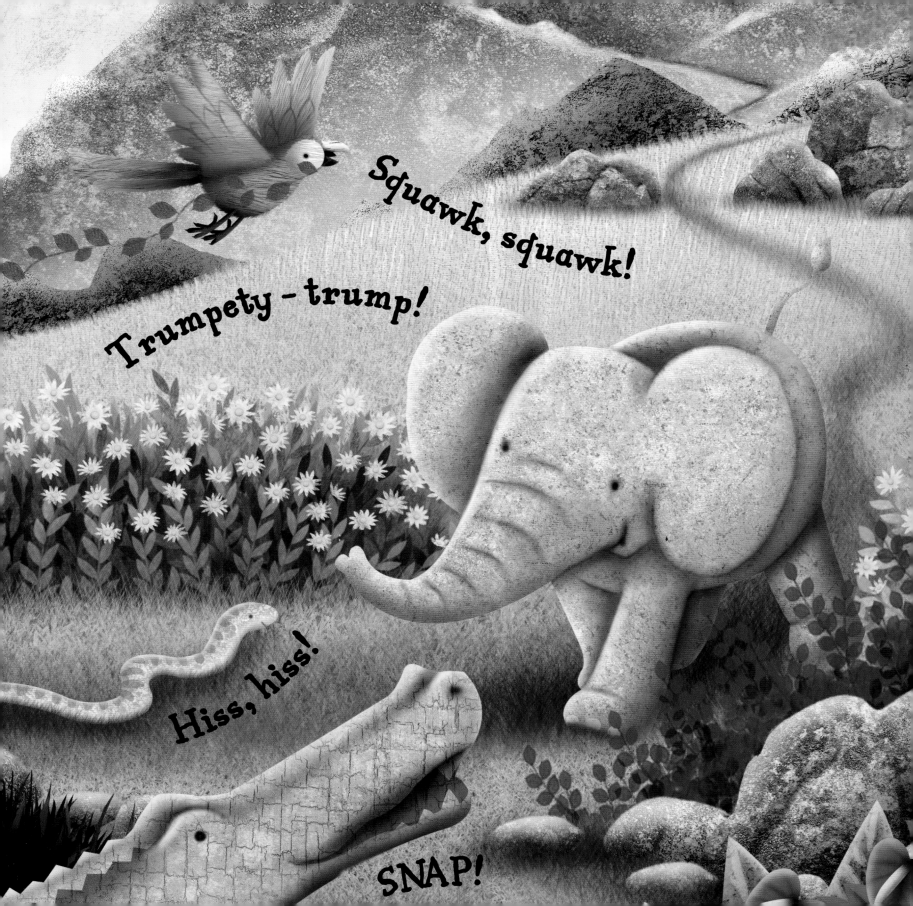

Those jungle animals made so much noise
as they passed by Lion's quiet, cool cave.

Sleepy Lion leapt out and gave a great big **ROAR!**
Then everyone stopped and there wasn't a sound.

Then, from the jungle came a rustle
and a bustle and a rumble and a thunder.
The trees shook and the ground shook
and there was a **very loud TRUMPET!**

It was Little Elephant's
mummy and daddy.

"Where were you?" asked Daddy Elephant, flapping his ears.
"With all my new friends," replied Little Elephant.
"We're having a jungle parade!"

Snake went **hiss** and Parrot gave a **squawk**.
Oo-oo went Monkey and Hippo went **glug**.
Snap went Crocodile and **ROAR** went Lion.

Then, one by one, the animals said goodbye to Little Elephant and his trumpeting little trunk.

Trumpety-trump!

Glug, glug!

Trumpety-trump!

Goodbye!